GUARDIAN
OF THE
FROSTHEART

Also By C. N. Noble

The Orphaned King, book one in The Chronicles of Mythandria.

Zeerian Creatures Field Guide. A companion guide to The Orphaned King.

Falling for Evil, a featured story in the multi-author anthology, Romancing The Rogue.

Frost & Starlight, a featured story in the multi-author anthology, A Bite of Winter & a Sip of Trouble.

GUARDIAN
OF
FROSTHEART

C. N. NOBLE

Dedication

To the frazzled raccoon gals and their insatiable desire to support and uplift others--especially the lovely Sophea Chan. Thank you.

Chapter 1

Liora walked beside Kaldor through the lively streets of Thaldridar's capital, her platinum hair peeking from beneath her fur-lined hood. She brushed her gloved fingers along the edges of the market stalls, her bright blue eyes shining with curiosity as she took in the sights around her. "You know," she said, her voice light and full of wonder, "there's something about the Winter Solstice Festival that just fills the air with magic. The snowflakes swirling around, the sound of the fiddler's song, and the laughter of the children... It's like the whole kingdom comes alive, even in the cold."

Kaldor wasn't much of a conversationalist while on duty—and Liora had only been in his presence while he was. She was used to his quiet, expressionless demeanor. Though, she had seen glimpses of his true character bleed through from time to time.

She inhaled deeply, letting the sweet, warm scents of spiced cider and roasted chestnuts fill her lungs. "The smell of chestnuts roasting in the air," she continued, "and the way the lanterns glow in the frost-covered streets—it's like they're lighting up the very soul of Thaldridar. It's such a contrast to the harsh winter, don't you think?" She smiled softly, glancing back at Kaldor as they walked. "I think it's a reminder of just how resilient our people are. Even in the hardest of times, we still find a way to celebrate, to bring warmth into the world."

Trailing a step behind, Kaldor moved with the precision of a soldier. His tall, broad-shouldered frame was impossible to miss, even in the shifting crowd. Citizens instinctively parted around him, treating him less as a man and more as a barrier—immovable and imposing. The faint breeze caught his platinum hair streaked with dark gray, the strands shimmering faintly in the enchanted light above. His sharp features—defined by a square jaw and piercing brown eyes, so rare among Thaldridarians—remained fixed in unwavering focus, scanning the crowd for any potential threat. One hand rested lightly on the pommel of his sword, the ease of the motion betraying years of discipline.

"Your ears appear to be cold, Captain," Liora observed, her voice carrying just enough mischief to pull his attention.

Kaldor's expression didn't waver, though the tips of his ears—already a deep pink from the chill—seemed to flush a shade darker.

"Perhaps you should make use of the hood resting at the base of your neck," she continued, her blue eyes gleaming with playful intent. "Or is it that your abnormally large arms can't quite manage to reach?"

"It's an intentional choice," Kaldor replied evenly, his tone calm despite her teasing. "A hood would disrupt my peripheral view, your highness."

Liora glanced over her shoulder, her platinum braid shifting beneath her hood. "You know," she said lightly, her teasing tone undeterred, "you could try relaxing for once. Maybe buy a potion or two, pick up a trinket for someone special?"

Her playful smile deepened as she caught his gaze. The frost-dappled light reflected in her bright eyes, and for a fleeting moment, she thought she saw his lips twitch—almost a smile, but not quite.

"Assuming," she added, turning her attention back to the bustling street, "you even know how to have fun."

Kaldor didn't break stride, his expression as stoic as ever. "My duty isn't to enjoy the market, Princess. It's to ensure your safety."

Liora sighed dramatically. "Yes, yes, the noble, ever-vigilant captain of the royal guard. But surely even you have hobbies, Kaldor. Or is brooding your only pastime?"

"I don't brood," he replied, his voice calm and even, though his brow furrowed slightly, betraying a flicker of irritation.

She turned her head just enough to catch his eye. Mischief glinted in her gaze. "Oh, you absolutely brood. You're brooding right now."

Kaldor's lips twitched — so faintly it might have gone unnoticed, but Liora caught the fleeting crack in his armor. "I'm observing," he corrected, his deep brown eyes already sweeping the crowd again.

"Observing," Liora echoed with mock seriousness, pausing to glance at a stall of enchanted scarves. She draped a shimmering blue one over her shoulders and turned to him, her expression playful. "Observe this. What do you think? Does it bring out my eyes?"

Kaldor hesitated, his gaze flicking to the scarf before quickly looking away, his posture stiffening ever so slightly. Liora's stomach fluttered at the momentary vulnerability in his expression, but it was gone just as quickly, replaced by his usual composure.

"It's...fine," he said at last, his tone deliberately neutral.

"Fine?" Liora tilted her head, feigning offense. "That's the best you can do? I'm crushed, truly."

"You're impossible," Kaldor muttered, his square jaw tightening, though there was a faint warmth creeping into his voice.

"And you're too easy to tease," she said with a grin, tossing the scarf back to the merchant with a wink. "One day, Kaldor, I'm going to make you smile. A real one. Not that stern half-frown you wear like armor."

He didn't reply, but as they continued down the frosty street, the corner of his mouth twitched again, and Liora decided it was a victory — however small.

For all his stoic professionalism, she knew there was more to him than he let on. And if peeling away his layers was the only rebellion she could get away with, she'd take it.

Liora slowed her steps, letting the festive energy wash over her. She pulled her fur-lined cloak snugly around her delicate frame, though the cold barely registered beneath the weight of her thoughts. The Winter Solstice was a time of joy and renewal, yet for her, it only served as a reminder of what might lay ahead—a burden she wasn't sure she was ready to bear.

"You know," Liora said, sidestepping closer to him with a playful lilt in her voice, "if I didn't know better, I'd think you were immune to fun. Is there a potion for that?"

Kaldor didn't immediately look at her, his attention still on the crowd. When he finally glanced her way, his mouth pressed into a thin line, though she swore she caught the faintest flicker of amusement in his eyes. "My immunity to 'fun,' as you call it, is what keeps you safe, Princess."

"Oh, please." Liora rolled her eyes, her boots crunching softly on the snow-dusted cobblestones as she gestured to the lively stalls around them. "What's safer than a marketplace full of happy people? Unless you think the pastry vendor is hiding a dagger in his scones."

Kaldor's lips twitched, almost imperceptibly, as he returned his gaze to the bustling square. "I don't trust pastries with too much filling," he muttered, his tone so dry that Liora burst out laughing.

"That might be the closest thing to humor I've heard from you," she teased, still grinning.

"I don't 'do' humor," he replied, though his voice had softened.

"No kidding." She linked her arm through his briefly, giving it a gentle squeeze before letting go when she felt his posture stiffen. Her smile faltered, and for a fleeting moment, she wondered if it was because he didn't want her to get the wrong idea.

Her steps slowed as her gaze drifted toward the children dancing around the ribbon-adorned pole, their carefree laughter ringing above the chatter. The music carried through the crisp air, wrapping the scene in a warmth that defied the chill. "Do you ever relax, Kaldor?" she asked, her voice quieter now, more curious than teasing. "I don't think I've ever seen you let your guard down. Not even for a moment."

Kaldor didn't answer right away, his brow furrowing slightly as he seemed to weigh his response. Finally, he said, "Relaxation isn't a luxury I can afford." His voice was steady, but there was something underneath it—something guarded.

"Not even for yourself?" she pressed, tilting her head to catch his expression.

He met her gaze, his sharp features momentarily softening. The tip of his ears, pink from the cold, gave him a fleeting vulnerability she wasn't used to seeing. "My comfort doesn't matter, Princess. The kingdom does."

Liora sighed, a wistful smile tugging at her lips. "You are the impossible one, Kaldor." She brushed a strand of her platinum hair back as a snowflake landed on her lashes, the chill a sharp contrast to the warmth blossoming in her chest.

6

With a teasing glint in her eyes, she added, "I'll figure out what you're hiding behind that frown someday. My guess? It's either a wicked sense of humor or an embarrassing love for pastry-filled scones."

Kaldor didn't reply immediately, his gaze returning to the crowd. The festival's cheer surrounded them—the flickering lanterns, the singing, the dancing—and for the briefest moment, she swore the corner of his mouth quirked up. Just a fraction.

Liora couldn't help but feel victorious. "Ah, there it is," she said triumphantly. "Progress."

Her smile grew as she turned her attention back to the crowd, but the weight of her own responsibilities lingered at the edges of her mind. The Frostheart Stone, though safe for now, would soon demand more of her than she had ever given before. For generations, the royal women of Thaldridar had been the only ones gifted with magic—an inheritance that came not just with power, but with responsibility. Before her passing, the queen had warned Liora many times that being born with magic didn't guarantee the Stone's acceptance. The Frostheart chose its own Guardian, binding them to its immense power and weighty demands.

Liora's magic had grown stronger in recent weeks, an undeniable sign that her time was coming. But the role of Guardian wasn't something she could claim on her own. It was a trial of endurance, will, and spirit—a bond forged only if the Stone deemed her worthy. And even then, the cost would be steep. She had seen it in her mother's weary eyes at the end of her days. The queen had held a graceful poise that masked years of silent sacrifice.

"I'll face it when the time comes," Liora murmured to herself, her resolve hardening. For now, there was still time to enjoy what little peace the Winter Solstice offered. Time to tease Kaldor and savor the moments before her destiny became her reality.

"You've gone quiet," Kaldor observed, his deep voice breaking through her thoughts.

Liora glanced at him, startled. "Just thinking," she replied, forcing a faint smile.

"About the Stone?" he asked, his perceptive gaze meeting hers.

She hesitated, then nodded. "It's a lot to carry, knowing what might come. But I'll face it." Her hood fell to her shoulders as she turned to look up at him. Icy air stung her skin and her chin chattered. "How did you know?"

Kaldor, using both of his hands, reached around and pulled her hood back up into place. "There aren't many subjects capable of quieting your enthusiasm," Kaldor said with an empathetic expression. "Knowing you, and I do, you'll beat whatever comes at you." His tone was firm, leaving no room for doubt. "You're stronger than you think, Princess."

The confidence in his voice steadied her in a way few things could. "Thank you," she said softly, her breath mingling with the frosty air.

Chapter 2

The music swirled around them again, the joyful laughter of children ringing through the square. For a brief moment, Liora allowed herself to embrace the simple joys of the festival, letting the weight of what was to come slip to the back of her mind. A bright smile spread across her face as the vibrant energy of the crowd filled her with warmth. She clapped her hands in time with the music and, caught up in the moment, impulsively looped her arm through Kaldor's.

For a fleeting instant, the contact felt completely natural, warm—even comfortable. But then, she felt Kaldor's posture stiffen, the tension in his body unmistakable. Her heart skipped a beat as she quickly pulled away, her smile faltering.

Had she misstepped? The thought flickered through her

mind, unbidden and frustrating. Perhaps he didn't want her to get the wrong idea. Though a part of her argued that it was too late for that—her feelings for Kaldor had long since shifted into something deeper than mere friendship.

But Kaldor never let his guard down long enough for their relationship to move beyond its carefully maintained boundaries. Even now, he stood rigid, his shoulders squared, his expression unreadable, as if the moment hadn't happened at all.

Liora pushed the thought aside, forcing a smirk back onto her lips, though a quiet uncertainty lingered beneath the surface.

Kaldor's sharp eyes caught movement in the shadow of a nearby alley. Liora followed his gaze, her playful demeanor faltering for a moment.

"What is it?" she asked quietly.

"Nothing yet," Kaldor replied, his tone serious once more. "But stay close."

"Always," she said softly, her teasing smile returning as they continued down the snow-dusted streets. Though she respected his sense of duty, she couldn't help but wish he'd let his guard down, just for a moment. Not for the sake of the festival, but for himself.

Before Kaldor could respond to Liora's teasing grin, a sudden gust of icy wind surged through the bustling market, extinguishing the magical lanterns overhead in an instant. The crowd froze, their cheerful chatter replaced by hushed murmurs and uneasy glances. Darkness swallowed the festive glow, leaving only the silvery shimmer of snowflakes catching faint moonlight.

Kaldor straightened, his entire posture sharpening like a drawn blade. "Stay close," he ordered, his voice low but firm. Without hesitation, he moved through the throng, his presence parting the crowd like a tide.

Liora followed, her heart pounding as instincts screamed something was wrong. "What is it?" she asked, trying to match his brisk pace.

"Magic," Kaldor muttered grimly, his eyes narrowing as he scanned the shadows ahead. "Something dark."

They wove through the stunned crowd, heading toward an alley where Kaldor had felt a pull earlier. Snow swirled heavier here, the flakes almost luminous in the dim light. That was when they saw it—a faint glow pulsing against the pristine white of the snowbank near a stack of weathered barrels.

"What is that?" Liora breathed, moving closer despite the sinking feeling in her gut.

Kaldor stepped in front of her, raising a hand to halt her approach. "Stay back."

"Oh, come on," she retorted, slipping past him before he could stop her. She crouched by the faint glow, brushing the snow aside. "A communication crystal," Liora murmured, her fingers trembling as she revealed the object beneath the snow. It glowed with an eerie crimson light—far too vivid and unnatural for a Thaldridar crystal, which should have been icy blue. Her breath caught in her chest as she held it in her hands. The communication crystals were unique to each kingdom,

11

each one a distinct color to make it easy to identify its origin. Its faint glow pulsed rhythmically, almost as if alive.

Kaldor moved closer, his gaze narrowing as he took in the strange hue. "This isn't Thaldridar's."

"No," Liora replied quietly, her heart pounding. "It's not." She could feel the unease creeping through her, a warning tugging at her instincts. "But whose is it?"

Kaldor crouched beside her, his expression darkening. "Careful, Princess. These aren't left behind by accident."

She ignored his warning, her fingers trembling slightly as she picked it up. The moment her hand touched its surface, the crystal flared brighter, and an image flickered to life above it—a hazy, ghostly projection.

Both froze as the figure came into focus. It was Prince Eryk.

"Eryk?" Liora whispered, her voice barely audible over the wind.

The image was blurry and distorted, but there was no mistaking the desperation in Eryk's expression. His lips moved as if forming words, but no sound accompanied the vision. Then, the image shifted—a vague, shadowy figure loomed behind him before the projection abruptly vanished, leaving only the faint glow of the crystal.

Kaldor was the first to speak, his tone hard as steel. "It's a message."

Liora turned to him, her stomach twisting. "A message for what? What does this mean?"

"I don't know," Kaldor admitted, his brow furrowing as he rose to his feet. "But we're going to find out." He extended a hand to help her up, his protective instincts flaring anew. "Let's go."

An icy chill crept down Liora's spine, stopping her in her tracks. Her breath clouded the air as dread clawed at her chest. She turned to Kaldor, her voice tight with urgency.

"Something's wrong. We have to go to the Frostheart Stone—now."

Kaldor's eyes narrowed, his focus sharpening as if he, too, felt the ominous shift. Without hesitation, he nodded, and they broke into a run, their boots crunching against frost-laden cobblestones. The festive hum of the marketplace faded behind them, replaced by the cold, echoing silence of the central square.

The towering spires of Thaldridar's ancient temple loomed ahead, the sacred site where the Frostheart Stone had been kept for generations. The magical lanterns that usually bathed the square in a soft glow flickered erratically, their light dimming with every step closer.

Liora's chest tightened as they approached the stone's resting place—a pedestal carved from ancient ice, shimmering with runes that pulsed faintly in rhythm with the stone's magic. Only now, the light was gone.

She stumbled to a halt, her worst fear confirmed. The Frostheart Stone was gone.

"No," she whispered, her voice trembling as she stared at the empty pedestal. Frost crept outward from the base, spreading like veins through the cobblestones, an eerie reminder of the power the stone held.

Kaldor moved swiftly, his expression grim as he examined the area. His hand hovered near the hilt of his sword, though no immediate threat was visible. "This isn't a coincidence," he said, his voice low and tense. "Someone planned this."

Their eyes met, a shared unease passing between them. The same thought hovered unspoken—a suspicion that Prince Eryk might somehow be involved. Kaldor's jaw tightened, but before he could voice it, Liora shook her head vehemently, her voice firm. "No. Eryk would never. He's too honorable to do anything that would put our people at risk, let alone condemn them to such a fate."

Kaldor didn't argue, though his eyes remained shadowed with doubt. "I hope you're right," he said at last, his tone guarded. "But we can't ignore the possibility—especially with the message."

Liora knelt by the pedestal, her fingertips brushing the faint frost. "Without the Stone, the kingdom's balance—its magic— it's vulnerable." She looked up at Kaldor, her eyes blazing with determination. "We have to find it before it's too late."

"Agreed," Kaldor replied, his tone steady but firm. He surveyed the square, his trained eyes searching for anything out of place. "But whoever took it couldn't have gone far. The Stone's power would draw too much attention in the open."

Liora rose to her feet, a mix of fear and resolve coursing through her. "Then we'll start here. Someone must have seen something—heard something."

Kaldor hesitated for a fraction of a second, his protective instincts warring with the urgency of the moment. Finally, he gave a curt nod. "We'll search the market, question anyone who might have been near. But if things escalate, I'm taking you back to the castle."

Liora clenched her fists, biting back a retort. She knew his concern came from a place of loyalty, but the kingdom's safety was more important than her own. "Let's just find it, Kaldor. We don't have time to argue."

Together, they turned back toward the town, their mission clear but the path ahead shrouded in uncertainty. The Frostheart Stone's absence wasn't just a theft — it was a harbinger of something far darker.

Kaldor's jaw tightened as he stepped back from the pedestal, his gaze sweeping the square with military precision. Without a word, he reached for the Thaldridar horn at his belt — a polished instrument etched with intricate runes that gleamed faintly even in the dim light. He raised it to his lips and blew a deep, resonant note that echoed through the icy streets like a warning bell.

Chapter 3

The sound of the Thaldridar horn carried over the marketplace and beyond, cutting through the festive din and drawing immediate attention. Within moments, armored figures began to emerge from the shadows of the square and surrounding alleys, the royal guards responding with swift discipline.

As the first guards reached him, Kaldor wasted no time. His voice was clear and commanding. "The Frostheart Stone has been stolen. Spread out and search the city—every alley, every shop, every shadow. Speak to the merchants and the festival-goers. Someone must have seen or heard something."

One of the guards, a young man with frost still clinging to his shoulders, nodded sharply. "Yes, Captain. Do we have any suspects?"

Kaldor shook his head, his brow furrowed. "Not yet. Focus on anyone acting suspiciously or seen fleeing the area. Move quickly. We cannot afford delay."

The guards saluted and dispersed into the city, their boots crunching against the frost-covered cobblestones as they moved with purpose.

Liora watched them fan out, a mix of hope and unease swirling in her chest. "Do you think they'll find anything?" she asked softly, her voice carrying an edge of desperation.

Kaldor turned to her, his expression unreadable but his tone steady. "They will. The thief couldn't have gotten far, not with the Stone. It's too powerful to conceal easily."

Liora nodded, drawing in a shaky breath. She could see the weight of responsibility pressing on him, the way he carried it in his squared shoulders and clenched jaw. But she refused to let herself falter now. "Then let's not waste time. We'll search, too."

He hesitated, the protector in him bristling at the thought of her walking into danger. But the fire in her eyes left no room for argument. Finally, he took hold of her hand and stared firmly into her eyes. "Stay close to me."

She didn't dare contest. "I will follow your lead."

Kaldor raised a brow. "That would be a first." he grumbled just loud enough for the princess to hear.

The crowded streets hummed with the energy of a city in turmoil, but Kaldor remained focused, guiding Liora swiftly through the mass of people. His hand, strong and steady around hers, never faltered, even though the urgency of their mission weighed heavily on him.

They reached the palace's side door, its unassuming appearance offering a temporary sanctuary from prying eyes. Kaldor's grip tightened as they moved through the shadows, bypassing the main entrance, where the royal guard had already gathered in response to the disappearance of the stone.

"This way," he murmured, nodding toward the narrow hallway leading to the armory.

The city outside the castle walls was alive with murmurs and hurried footsteps, but within the narrow, dimly lit hallways, there was only silence.

Liora glanced up at him, her expression unreadable, but the tension in her posture told him everything he needed to know. She was more than aware of what he intended to do.

"Why the side door, Kaldor?" Her voice was soft, but it held a quiet challenge. "Not the front gates?"

Kaldor's lips pressed into a firm line as he guided her through the door. "The front entrance is swarming with guards, Lior—your highness," he quickly corrected. "This is a faster route to your safety."

"My safety?"

"You'll be safer inside the castle with the king."

She stopped, jerking him to a halt as she pulled against his grasp, her gaze piercing and resolute. "No." The word was simple but heavy, like an anchor. "I won't stay behind."

Kaldor's expression darkened, his jaw tightening. "You're not trained for this. You can't—"

"I'm not helpless, Kaldor," she interrupted, her tone rising slightly with the frustration that had been brewing inside her. "I'm not a child you can just lock away when there's danger."

"You are the king's daughter," he said, trying to keep his voice steady. "Your place is with him, safe within the castle walls."

Liora's eyes flashed with determination. She took a step forward, closing the distance between them, and Kaldor felt a jolt in his chest. "If you think for one second that I'll sit idly by while my brother is out there—while our kingdom is at risk—you're wrong. I'll sneak out if I have to. I'll—"

"Don't even think it," he quickly interrupted with a stern expression. Kaldor's brow furrowed, and his eyes narrowed in a mixture of frustration and something she couldn't quite place. He glanced at her—just a flicker of a look—but she could see it. The conflict. The worry. It was there, hidden beneath the surface, in the tight set of his jaw and the way his shoulders stiffened. "I can't protect you, find the prince, and bring home the stone," he muttered, his words edged with a deep concern that made her chest tighten.

Liora held his gaze, refusing to back down. "I'm going," she said in a firm tone. "Besides, I am the only Thaldridarian magically connected to the Stone. I'm the only chance you have of getting it back."

For a long moment, he didn't speak, and the air between them felt thick with unspoken words. Liora watched him, noting the subtle ways his expression shifted—how his eyes softened just slightly, like he was trying to hold something back. She knew him too well. She had seen it before, even if he tried to hide it.

She tilted her chin up defiantly, her blue eyes never leaving his. "If you don't take me with you, I'll find a way to follow. I swear it, Kaldor. I'll do it myself."

Liora noticed the flicker of tension in Kaldor's jaw, his usually measured voice carrying an uncharacteristic edge as he muttered, "Why must you make things so complicated?"

Liora crossed her arms across her bodice with a look of defiance.

"If I take you with me," he began, his voice lower, more strained than he intended, "I won't hesitate to put your safety above all else. You, Princess, are my priority. I will come back without the stone or the prince if it means bringing you home unharmed."

Liora's breath caught in her chest. There it was — the unsaid truth. As a Thaldridar guard, Kaldor swore to protect the kingdom first and then the crown. It wasn't just about finding the prince or the stone. It was about Kaldor having feelings for her — about him looking at her like she was everything to him, even if he wouldn't admit it aloud. Even if he would never allow himself to say the words that burned in the space between them.

"I know." Liora closed the space between them, her fingers gently grasping the edge of his fur cloak. Her heart pounded as she looked up into his eyes, feeling the depth of the unspoken bond between them. "I trust you."

Kaldor stiffened at her touch, his breath catching in his

throat before he could stop it. "Liora..." His voice was raw, vulnerable, filled with all the things he had hidden for so long.

A surge of warmth flooded Liora's chest. That was the first time he had ever said her name. Her gaze softened, the edges of her heart curling toward him. Slowly, almost instinctively, her hand found his once more, fingers brushing against his in a silent promise. The world around them seemed to fade away, leaving only the two of them in that quiet moment.

His hand tightened around hers. "We will leave together," he said quietly, his voice low and full of resolve. "But promise me," he said with a returning firm gaze, "Whatever I ask you to do, no matter how trivial it may seem, you will do it."

She raised a brow at his request.

"I need to know that you'll do as I ask, princess. Even if I have to carry you."

Liora smiled, a soft, knowing smile that held both mischief and warmth. "You might need to. But if you're truly going to keep me safe, Kaldor, you'll have to learn to trust me as much as I trust you."

He hesitated. The weight of her words settled in the space between them, and Kaldor finally nodded, the barest hint of a smile tugging at his lips. "Then I'll trust you."

Voices of guards walking through the narrow passageways cut through her thoughts and immediately drew Kaldor's attention.

"Gather what you need. I will be back in a moment," he said, his tone steady, but there was a flicker of urgency in his eyes. It was a look she had grown used to seeing over the years, but tonight it carried something more — a deeper sense of worry she couldn't ignore. Kaldor hastily left her side, disappearing around a corner. A moment later, Liora could hear him and a couple of others talking but not what was being said.

Liora moved swiftly, her hands steady as she selected a short blade from the weapons rack. It was light enough to wield easily in the dense wilderness, where speed would be as important as strength. She grabbed a satchel and began filling it with supplies: dried meats, a flask of water, a small vial of healing herbs, and flint. Her fingers brushed over a map of Thalridar on the wall, and her gaze lingered on the northern wilderness — the last place Eryk had been seen. Her stomach twisted. Could he really be out there alone? She took a deep breath, pushing the fear aside. She had already suffered the loss of her mother, she wasn't about to lose him as well.

Kaldor returned and hurriedly moved through the armory with practiced ease as he gathered his own gear. When he turned toward her, he saw her staring at the map on the wall. His expression was unreadable, but his eyes softened just slightly as he glanced at the map, his lips tightening.

"The north gates are several days' travel from here," he said, his voice low. "We'll need to move quickly if we're going to track him before it's too late."

Liora nodded, the weight of his words settling in her chest. "Then let's not waste any more time," she said, her voice steady despite the nerves twisting in her stomach.

Kaldor's gaze flickered to the door. For a moment, he hesitated — just a heartbeat — but then he met her eyes again, a flicker of resolve passing between them. "Once we leave, there's no turning back."

Liora swallowed hard, pushing the fear away, and raised her chin. "I'm ready."

Kaldor gave a small nod, his expression hardening as he turned to lead the way. Liora followed closely behind, her steps quick and purposeful. As they moved through the shadowed halls of the palace, the quiet weight of the adventure ahead pressing in around them. Every sound, every creak of the floor beneath their feet felt amplified, and with each step, the distance between them and the unknown dangers of the wilderness grew smaller.

They reached the palace gates, and Kaldor didn't hesitate. His hand released hers, and he gave a sharp whistle that echoed through the stillness. From the shadows of the stables, three soldiers emerged on the backs of three strange horse-like creatures. With them, two additional creatures. Their sleek forms cut through the snow like living wind. These were Froststeeds, creatures as rare as the auroras that danced over the northern skies. Each stood taller than any ordinary horse, their silvery, shimmering coats seeming to blend with the snow around them. Their manes rippled like spun ice, glittering faintly under the moonlight. Strong, feathered hooves left no trace in the snow, and their deep-set, pale blue eyes glowed softly, betraying their magical nature. Froststeeds were bred for the harsh winters of Thaldridar, capable of traveling great distances without rest, food, or water. They thrived in the cold, their breath visible in the frosty air as they exhaled in soft, rhythmic puffs.

Kaldor approached the nearest one, his broad shoulders cutting an imposing figure against the glow of the froststeeds' shimmering coats. He ran a gloved hand along the stallion's neck, murmuring words that Liora couldn't make out, before turning toward her. The mare, smaller but no less graceful, lowered her head as Liora stepped forward, her icy mane sparkling faintly.

Liora reached a tentative hand toward the creature, her breath catching as its silken muzzle brushed against her palm. "They're magnificent," she whispered, her voice barely carrying above the stillness.

Kaldor nodded, his gaze steady as he turned back to her. "They're the fastest we have. You'll need her strength for what's ahead." Without waiting for her response, he stepped closer, his strong hands reaching for her waist.

Before Liora could protest, Kaldor's firm grip lifted her effortlessly off the ground. The sudden motion sent her heart racing, though she wasn't entirely sure it was from the movement alone. He placed her gently into the Froststeed's saddle, the gesture efficient but undeniably careful, as if he'd considered her comfort more than she had.

"Thank you," she murmured, glancing down at him.

Kaldor didn't reply, his expression unreadable as he adjusted the reins in her hands. "Hold tight," he said finally, his voice low but steady.

She nodded, her gaze lingering on him as he mounted his own Froststeed in one fluid motion. His presence was commanding, as natural on the majestic creature as it was within the palace walls. The Froststeed beneath him shifted slightly, its luminous eyes watching him as if waiting for a command.

Kaldor turned to her, his brown eyes meeting hers. "Stay close," he said, his tone firm but not without a thread of care woven through it.

"I will," she replied softly, gripping the reins. At her urging, the Froststeed began to move, its hooves gliding soundlessly across the snow. She could feel the power thrumming beneath her, the creature's innate magic flowing like a steady current.

Chapter 4

The first sign of trouble came with the wind, sharp and biting, slicing through the mountain pass. Liora pulled her cloak tighter, feeling the chill seep through the layers of her clothing. The snow was coming down harder now, blurring the path ahead but the froststeeds pushed through with ease. Liora glanced at Kaldor, who seemed to be scanning the horizon with a practiced eye. Behind them, the other soldiers followed in grim silence.

Kaldor slowed his horse, turning to face the group. "Stay close. If we get separated in this, it'll be harder to regroup."

Liora nodded, her face already stinging from the wind's bite. She was used to the cold of Thalridar, but the storm seemed different today—angrier.

After a long silence, one of the soldiers, Halric, pointed ahead. "Commander, I see something—looks like a structure. Might be a cabin."

Kaldor's gaze hardened as he followed Halric's pointing finger. "I know it. It's a shelter I've used before. Stay alert."

Liora was surprised. "You've been out here before?"

He didn't answer at first, instead urging his horse forward with purpose. "Stay with me," he said over his shoulder.

They pressed on, and within moments, the dark outline of a cabin began to emerge from the storm's fury. The weathered structure was tucked against the rock face, barely visible.

"Halric, Maren, go check the perimeter. Rothar, help me with the horses," Kaldor ordered as he dismounted. The soldiers moved without hesitation, their boots crunching in the snow as they spread out.

Liora followed Kaldor up to the cabin. He wiped the snowy dusting away from the grimy window to peer inside. "It appears vacant." Kaldor went to the front door but it wouldn't open right away. He roughly tugged on the door handle twice and it finally swung ajar—revealing the darkened space within.

Liora's eyes quickly adjusted to the darkness. The home was a single small space but sturdy, with a few cracked wooden beams supporting the roof. A hearth sat cold and unused, but there were enough supplies scattered about for them to make use of.

Kaldor knelt by the hearth, his gloved hands brushing through the dry wood stacked nearby. "If we can get a fire going, we can wait out the storm here. The pass is too dangerous in weather like this."

Liora nodded, but as she reached for a few logs, Kaldor stopped her, his hand gently closing around hers. "No," he said softly, his gaze flicking to her lips, already tinged with blue. "You're freezing."

He rose to his feet, looking around the cabin until he found a battered chair in the corner. Without a word, he placed it by the fire. "Sit here while I get the fire going."

Liora didn't protest. She moved slowly to the chair, hugging her arms around herself as the chill from the storm clung to her bones.

Kaldor unclasped his cloak and draped it over her shoulders, his fingers lingering for just a moment longer than necessary. His face remained neutral, but there was something in the set of his jaw that told Liora he regretted bringing her along on this journey. That perhaps he thought her unfit for this harsh task.

She sank into the warmth of the chair, the cloak wrapping around her like a shield against the cold.

The fire crackled to life as Kaldor arranged larger logs atop the kindling. Liora watched the flames catch, the soft golden light casting flickering shadows against the walls. The warmth melted away the lingering chill from her cheeks, the sudden contrast making her skin tingle. She pulled her cloak tighter around her, the fur-lined edges brushing her jaw as she let the heat seep into her bones.

The glow of the fire danced across Kaldor's features,

softening the sharp angles of his jaw and the ever-present intensity in his deep brown eyes. For a fleeting moment, Liora allowed herself to simply watch him, her gaze tracing the way the light reflected off the streaks of platinum and gray in his hair. The rhythmic crackling of the wood filled the quiet space between them, a gentle harmony to the stillness of the night.

"You've done this before," Liora said softly, her voice almost lost in the hiss of the flames. She wasn't sure if she meant starting the fire or bearing the weight of their journey with such stoic composure.

Kaldor glanced up, his eyes meeting hers across the glow of the fire. The warmth there startled her, a flicker of something unspoken softening his normally guarded expression. "More times than I can count," he replied evenly, though his tone carried a quiet reassurance.

"Always the soldier," she murmured, a faint smile tugging at her lips. "You make even this seem effortless."

His gaze lingered on her for a moment longer, the firelight catching a hint of something deeper in his eyes—something that made her heart skip a beat. Then he looked away, settling into a more comfortable sitting position on the floor. "Effortless isn't always what it seems," he said, his voice low but steady.

Cool air brushed the back of her ankles, sending a chill up Liora's legs. She stood, moved the chair back, and sat at his side—their hips touching. After a moment of sitting as still as a statue, Kaldor leaned toward her, placing his palm on the floor behind her. With her eyes fixed on the flames, she could feel him gazing at her. But she stayed where she was, letting the unspoken words linger in the crackling silence.

The door opened loudly and Rothar entered, stomping his snow covered boots and brushing off his cloak with a grunt.

Kaldor immediately shifted away from Liora as if he didn't want to be seen so intimately close to the princess.

"All clear," Rothar reported, his eyes scanning the small cabin with an appreciative look. "Not exactly a palace, but it'll do."

Liora smiled faintly, the firelight dancing in her tired eyes.

Kaldor stood, his gaze distant as he surveyed the room. "It's more than we expected, given the storm."

Halric and Maren stomped their shoes as they trailed up behind Rothar. What warmth the tiny shelter had been holding was now escaping through the open door. Liora leaned toward the fire, stretching her frozen fingers toward its heat. She was surprised by how grateful she felt for the small, sheltered space. For all their urgency and the bitter cold outside, there was a strange sense of calm here.

"Good work, Halric," Kaldor said, giving the soldier who had first spotted the cabin an approving nod. "I'd all but forgotten about this place."

"Could've sworn this place was abandoned long ago," Maren commented from across the room, unwrapping her scarf.

Kaldor looked over at her. "It was. I used to take refuge here when I was younger." His voice softened as he added, almost to himself, "Before everything changed." The weight of his words settled in the air between them, but no one pressed him further.

With a roaring fire, Rothar and Halric began to unpack rations. Maren, always the practical one, started to check the cabin's few shelves for anything useful — an old lantern, a few spare blankets. Liora glanced at Kaldor, who had already begun preparing to rest for the night. He stretched his legs out near the fire, his posture still rigid despite the comfort.

"What were you like as a child" Liora asked quietly, in hopes of a light conversation to bide time. She could see a heaviness appear in his eyes — something that had followed him from the past.

Kaldor didn't answer right away. He stared into the fire, the light flickering off his face. "I didn't have much of a childhood," he said at last. "I was six when my family was taken by the Winter King's forces. My parents... my sister..." His voice broke for a moment, but he quickly steadied it. "That's why I fight. To make sure no one else has to lose everything the way I did."

Liora felt a pang in her chest, her own grief stirred by the rawness in his words. "I understand. When my mother passed away, the world seemed empty." Her voice trailed off as the memories rushed in, unbidden.

"I'm sorry," Kaldor said, his gaze flicking to her.

"And I, for you," she said softly, meeting his eyes.

The fire crackled between them, both of them lost in their thoughts. The storm outside seemed to intensify, but the warmth of the cabin and the flickering light held it at bay.

"We'll find your brother," Kaldor said, his voice firm, as if staking a claim in the storm.

Liora nodded, though a part of her wondered if they would find him in time.

The wind howled outside, but inside the cabin, the storm felt distant, almost manageable. The small posse stayed like that for hours, the fire dwindling to embers, until Rothar finally spoke again.

"Storm's letting up. We'll be able to move soon," Kaldor said, his voice cutting through the quiet tension.

His expression hardened as he glanced toward the dark peaks ahead. "We don't have much time. Get the horses ready. We'll head out as soon as the snow clears enough to travel."

They moved quickly, gathering their belongings and preparing for the next leg of the journey. The storm had been brutal, but the mountains ahead loomed even more ominously, shrouded in shadows and danger. Liora stepped outside to help with the horses, pulling her cloak tightly around her shoulders. The biting cold stung her face, though the snow had eased, leaving the world strangely still. Too still. Her hand paused mid-motion, gripping the reins, as a low, guttural growl rippled through the air. The sound seemed to rise from the very cliffs around them, sending a chill down her spine. She froze, her hand instinctively moving to the hilt of her blade. The dim light of the fading storm shifted as something massive emerged from the gloom.

Towering above them was a beast, its colossal form forged

of ice and primal fury. The wolf-like creature stood at least fifteen feet tall, its body shimmering with layers of enchanted ice that reflected faint, pale light. Veins of frozen energy coursed beneath its crystalline surface, pulsing faintly with each slow, deliberate step.

The Frostbeast's head was monstrous, crowned with jagged ice spikes that jutted out like a savage crest. Its glowing blue eyes burned like frozen fire, locking onto the group with an unnatural intelligence that sent shivers racing down Liora's spine. Frosty breath billowed from its maw, lined with jagged shards of ice that caught the fading light of the storm.

Massive limbs ended in clawed hands that raked the frozen ground, each step gouging deep furrows into the snow-covered earth. A spiked, ice-encrusted tail lashed behind it, the sheer force of its movements cracking nearby rocks. Snow swirled around the beast, as though the remnants of the storm obeyed its will.

Kaldor stepped up beside Liora, his hands gripping his sword. His calm, measured tone belied the tension in his posture. "Stay close. This is it. We fight, or we don't get through."

Liora's pulse thundered in her ears as the Frostbeast advanced, its claws scraping against stone and ice with a sound that made her blood run cold. Maren appeared at her side, bow in hand, her face set with determination, while Rothar hefted his axe and Halric drew his sword, their stance unyielding.

The Frostbeast loomed closer, its glowing eyes fixed on them, and the air around it grew colder with every breath. For a brief moment, the world seemed to hold its breath, and then chaos erupted.

Chapter 5

The beast let out a bone-chilling roar, the sound reverberating through the valley and dislodging shards of ice from the cliffs above.

Rothar and Halric were already running toward them, weapons drawn. Maren followed, slinging her bow from her shoulder and nocking an arrow with swift precision.

"What in the depths is that?" Rothar demanded, his breath rising in clouds.

"A guardian," Kaldor replied grimly. "We've entered its territory."

Without warning, the beast charged. It moved with terrifying speed, its massive form barreling toward them.

"Scatter!" Kaldor barked, leaping into action.

The group split, each moving instinctively to flank the creature. Liora hesitated, her heart pounding in her chest as she took in its size and ferocity.

"Liora! We could use your help," Halric called, his tone a nervous mix of urgency and snark.

"Focus." Kaldor's voice sliced through the tension like steel, sharp and commanding, pulling her out of her spiraling thoughts.

She sucked in a breath, forcing herself to move. Raising her hands, she summoned the frost within her, feeling the magic surge to her fingertips. It was time to face the beast head-on. The air around her seemed to still as a shimmering wave of ice surged forth, coating the ground beneath the beast in a slick sheet. Its claws scrabbled for purchase, and it stumbled, giving the others an opening.

Rothar took the chance to swing his axe again, this time landing a solid blow to the creature's flank. It howled in pain, but the wound seemed to close almost instantly, the ice reforming over it.

"It's regenerating!" Maren called out, nocking another arrow.

Liora pushed forward, her magic flowing stronger now. She focused on the creature's legs, freezing them in place with sharp spikes of ice that climbed like vines. The strain was immediate, a sharp ache spreading through her chest, but she pressed on.

The beast thrashed violently, breaking free of her hold with a shattering crack. A sharp shard of ice flew toward her, but

Kaldor was there in an instant, his sword deflecting it with a metallic ring.

"Stay behind me," he ordered, his voice tight.

"I can help!" she protested, though her legs felt unsteady beneath her.

"And you'll help better alive," he snapped, his focus never wavering from the beast. Kaldor charged forward, his sword glowing faintly as he struck at the creature's chest. The impact sent a ripple of energy through the air, and for the first time, the beast faltered.

"Liora, we need more!" Kaldor called.

Gritting her teeth, Liora drew on the last reserves of her magic. Ice spiraled from her hands, encasing the beast's head in a thick layer of frost. The creature roared again, its movements slowing as the frost spread down its neck.

"Now!" she cried.

Halric and Rothar struck simultaneously, their weapons driving deep into the beast's exposed chest. With a final, anguished cry, the creature collapsed, its body shattering into a cascade of snow and ice.

The creature's remains glittered in the faint light of the storm as the group stood amidst the silence. Snowflakes swirled gently down around them, their delicate beauty a sharp contrast to the battle they had just survived. Liora's breaths came in ragged gasps, her legs trembling from exertion. The icy ache in her chest lingered—a reminder of the immense strain her magic had put on her.

Kaldor approached her, his sword sheathed but his

expression still tense. "Are you hurt?" he asked, his voice measured, though his eyes betrayed his worry.

"I'm fine," Liora said, though her voice wavered. She straightened, unwilling to show how much the battle had drained her. "It's nothing a little warmth won't fix."

His gaze lingered on her for a moment before shifting to the remains of the creature. Its shimmering shards had already begun to dissolve into the snow, leaving behind a single, faintly glowing fragment—a shard of ice that pulsed like a heartbeat.

Rothar crouched beside it, his brow furrowed. "What in the gods' name was that thing?"

"A guardian," Kaldor replied, his tone heavy. "The Frostheart Stone has protected this realm for generations, its magic bound to the balance of the land. That creature wasn't just guarding—it was born from that power, warped by the imbalance."

Liora shivered at his words, a deep unease settling in her chest. She stepped forward, her eyes fixed on the shard. "If it's tied to the Stone's magic, then it knew we were coming," she said softly. "It was protecting something."

She knelt, her hand hovering over the shard. The cold radiating from it was sharp and biting, but she couldn't look away. When her fingertips brushed its surface, a voice erupted in her mind, low and resonant:

Beware the Frostheart. Its power is not yours to wield.

Liora gasped, pulling her hand back as if burned. The shard fell to the ground, its glow dimming slightly.

Kaldor was at her side instantly. "What happened?"

"It spoke to me," Liora whispered, her voice trembling. "It warned me about the Frostheart Stone—that its power isn't ours to control."

"Then we need to find it before its magic spreads any further," Kaldor said grimly. "Whatever balance the Stone kept, it's starting to break, and that's putting the entire kingdom at risk."

The group exchanged uneasy glances but gathered their weapons without hesitation. The entrance to the cave yawned before them, dark and unwelcoming, but it was their only path forward.

As they stepped inside, the air turned colder still. Frost lined the walls in intricate patterns, glinting like diamonds in the faint light. Each step seemed to echo, the sound bouncing off the icy cavern and deepening the oppressive silence.

"Footprints," Maren murmured, pointing to the ground ahead.

Liora's heart skipped a beat. The tracks were unmistakable—human, and fresh enough that the snow hadn't yet reclaimed them. She knelt to inspect them, her fingers brushing against the frost-covered ground.

"It's him," she said quietly.

"Eryk," Kaldor agreed, his voice low. But there was no relief in his tone, only suspicion.

They pressed on, following the footprints deeper into the cavern. The walls seemed to pulse faintly, as if alive, and the air grew heavier with each step. Liora's magic stirred uneasily within her, as though it sensed the power ahead.

"What if the warning was true?" she murmured to herself, the words escaping before she could stop them.

Kaldor glanced back at her, his expression unreadable but his eyes briefly softening. "Whatever the truth is, we'll face it together. Keep moving."

And then, they saw it—a faint, unnatural glow emanating from deeper within the cave. The light grew stronger as they approached, revealing jagged shards of ice protruding from the walls, each glowing with the same eerie luminescence.

Kaldor raised a hand, signaling the group to stop. "Stay close," he said, his voice steady but tense. He turned to Liora, his gaze softening for just a moment. "No matter what happens, don't stray."

Liora nodded, her heart pounding. The Frostheart Stone had protected Thaldridar for centuries, its magic woven into the very fabric of their realm. But now, with its power untethered and stolen, she couldn't help but wonder what they would find waiting for them in the depths of this cavern—and whether they were prepared to face it.

As they rounded the next bend, the glow grew brighter, revealing a massive chamber at the heart of the cave. At its center stood a jagged crystalline spire, its surface pulsating with light but no sign of the Frostheart stone itself. Liora's breath caught in her throat, at the sight she found scattered around. The chamber was filled with signs of a struggle—broken pieces of equipment, fresh scorch marks, and blood smeared against the ice. And in the shadow of the glowing spire stood a figure, cloaked in tattered furs, their face obscured.

"Eryk," Liora whispered, her voice barely audible.

The figure didn't move, but the faintest chuckle echoed through the chamber, sending a shiver down her spine.

"Or worse," Kaldor murmured, his hand tightening around the hilt of his sword.

The Frostheart Stone's glow pulsed once, brighter than before, as though welcoming them — or warning them. The pulse cast strange, shifting shadows across the icy walls, bathing the chamber in an otherworldly glow.

Liora's breath hitched as she stepped closer. She couldn't tear her eyes away from the cloaked figure. Their stillness was more unnerving than any motion might have been.

"Eryk?" she called again, her voice trembling but loud enough to echo faintly.

The figure finally moved, tilting its head slightly toward her voice. A low chuckle escaped the shadows of the hood, faint but filled with an unsettling edge.

Liora's stomach twisted. That laugh wasn't her brother's.

"Liora, stay back," Kaldor warned, stepping in front of her with his sword at the ready.

Maren's bow creaked as she drew the string taut, her arrow aimed steadily at the figure. Rothar and Halric moved to flank Kaldor, their weapons gleaming in the Frostheart's eerie light.

The figure lifted a hand slowly, not in surrender but as if beckoning them closer. "You're too late," the voice rasped, distorted and unnatural. "The Frostheart belongs to me now."

Liora clenched her fists, anger and fear warring within her. "Who are you? What have you done with Prince Eryk?"

The figure didn't answer. Instead, the crystal spire flared violently, its light flooding the chamber with a cold so intense it burned. The jagged belfry seemed to hum, resonating with the figure's presence as cracks began to spread across its surface.

"Get back!" Kaldor barked, pushing Liora behind him just as the ground trembled beneath their feet.

The figure let out a low, menacing laugh, their form dissolving into a swirl of icy mist that whipped around the room. The glowing spire pulsed brighter, the chamber vibrating with its raw, unchecked power.

"We need to move!" Kaldor shouted, his voice cutting through the rising chaos.

But Liora's gaze remained fixed on the hypnotic pulsing of the spire, dread clawing at her chest. Whatever had been set into motion, she knew this was only the beginning.

Kaldor roughly pulled her to face him. "We're running out of time. We need to keep moving."

Chapter 6

The cave's stillness pressed heavily on Liora as they stepped deeper into its icy depths. The magical glow they had been surrounded by, had faded with the swirling mist— leaving the cavern dim and oppressive. The faint flicker of their torches illuminated jagged walls, and every breath crystallized in the frigid air. Liora wrapped her cloak tightly around her, though the cold was already bone deep.

"What if it's a trap?" Maren whispered, her voice barely carrying over the soft crunch of boots on frost.

"Everything about this is a trap," Rothar grunted. His axe rested against his shoulder, the edge gleaming faintly in the torchlight. "But we can't stop now."

Kaldor's steps were deliberate, his focus sharp as his eyes

swept the shadows ahead. He hadn't said much since they entered the cave, but Liora could feel the tension radiating from him. She followed closely, her fingers itching with the remnants of magic still simmering beneath her skin.

They came to a halt as the walls around them began to shimmer faintly under the torchlight. At first, it seemed like a trick of the ice, but then the shapes became clearer — patterns carved into the walls, their edges glittering like trapped starlight.

"Look at this," Liora murmured, stepping closer to trace the carvings with her fingers.

The group gathered around, their torches casting shifting light over the ancient mural. It depicted scenes from Thaldridar's history, though the images were foreign to Liora's eyes.

The first panel showed the Frostheart Stone cradled in the hands of a figure cloaked in light. Around her, the land seemed to flourish — forests grew, rivers flowed, and the sun shone brightly above.

"The Frostheart's magic," Halric said, his voice low. "It wasn't just protection. It gave life to this realm."

Maren's torch illuminated the next panel, where the Frostheart's glow had grown brighter. The figure now stood atop a frozen throne, and shadows began to creep into the corners of the scene.

"What's happening here?" Liora asked, frowning.

"Too much power," Kaldor said grimly, his tone heavy with understanding. "The Stone wasn't just protecting — it was controlling. And that control came with a cost."

The final panel was the most chilling. The Frostheart's light had turned harsh and cold, its glow consuming everything in its path. Forests lay in ruin, rivers frozen solid, and the kneeling figures from the first panel had become skeletal forms locked in ice.

Liora's stomach twisted as she stepped back, her torchlight shaking slightly. "The Stone didn't just protect—it destroyed when it wasn't controlled."

"Or when it was used by the wrong hands," Maren added, her voice laced with unease.

"That's what this is about," Rothar said, gesturing to the mural. "Whoever has the Stone isn't just trying to throw Thaldridar into chaos. They're trying to harness its power for themselves."

Kaldor's frown deepened. "And the prince might have helped them do it."

Liora whirled on him, her voice rising with indignation. "Eryk wouldn't betray Thaldridar! He wouldn't betray us!"

Kaldor met her gaze steadily, though his eyes softened slightly. "I want to believe that too, Liora. But fresh tracks and an abandoned cloak tell a different story," he said gesturing to the ground at their feet.

Liora's chest tightened as she stared at him, frustration and fear warring within her. She turned sharply, her gaze falling on the frost-covered ground where a familiar cloak lay half-buried. Her heart ached at the sight of it, the fur-lined edges unmistakable. She knelt, her trembling hands brushing the fabric.

"This doesn't mean anything," she whispered, though the words felt hollow. "He could've been forced," she argued, her voice trembling. "You don't know what he's been through, what—"

"You're right. I don't know," Kaldor interrupted, his voice calm but firm. "But neither do you. And until we do, we can't rule anything out."

Kaldor crouched beside her, his hand hesitating in the air before resting lightly on her shoulder. The touch sent a shiver through her, though not from the cold. "Princess," he said softly, his tone losing its usual edge. "I know this isn't easy. But if he's in trouble, we'll find him. If he's not..." He trailed off, his voice thick with the weight of what he didn't say.

She turned to face him, her heart aching at the way his eyes—usually so guarded—softened. "Do you think I'm naive?"

"No," he said firmly. "I think you're intelligent and brave. Braver than most." He tucked a loose strand of her hair behind her ear. "But you struggle, or are incapable of, seeing the worst parts of people. The parts that make us who we really are deep inside."

Their gazes held for a moment, and the air between them seemed to shift. The walls Kaldor kept so firmly in place were crumbling. The stoicism, the duty. Beneath it was a man who carried more than his share of burdens. A man who cared more deeply than he would ever admit.

Liora couldn't argue. He wasn't wrong. She loved people. She saw so much kindness, joy, and potential in everyone. It was a strength and a weakness.

His hand slipped away as he straightened, the moment breaking like a fragile thread. "We should keep moving."

Rothar's sharp voice cut through the rising tension. "We've got company."

The group spun toward the sound of approaching footsteps, their weapons raised. A figure emerged from the shadows, their appearance as unexpected as the guardian beast they had just fought.

"Hold!" the man said, raising his hands in a gesture of peace. His frame was thin beneath a heavy cloak, and round spectacles perched on the bridge of his nose. "I'm not here to fight."

"Who are you?" Kaldor demanded, his sword poised.

"Professor Garrick," the man replied, his voice calm but urgent. "Former royal scholar and, as fate would have it, someone who knows exactly what you're dealing with."

Liora's suspicion flared. "What are you doing here?"

Garrick adjusted his spectacles. "I've been following the Frostheart's trail since it was taken. I knew something was wrong when its magic began to surge across the realm. It disrupted the northern ley lines—a phenomenon no scholar could ignore."

"You expect us to believe you stumbled into this cave by coincidence?" Rothar asked skeptically.

"Hardly," Garrick replied. "I spent years studying the Frostheart. I know its power, its purpose, and its dangers. When I realized the ley lines led here, I couldn't ignore it.

My timing seems fortunate for you, though I assure you it's anything but."

"And what do you know about the Stone?" Liora pressed.

"It's not just a relic. It's a key," Garrick explained, his tone heavy. "The Frostheart doesn't just protect—it seals away a force that once nearly destroyed this world. If the wrong hands unlock that power…" He trailed off, his expression grim.

Kaldor lowered his sword slightly, his expression hard. "And you're here to stop that?"

"I'm here to help those who can," Garrick replied, his gaze shifting between the group. "If we don't act fast, the Frostheart's magic will undo everything Thaldridar has built."

The gravity of his words settled heavily over them.

"Then lead the way," Kaldor said after a long pause, his voice laced with determination.

As Garrick turned toward the deeper part of the cave, Liora lingered, her gaze falling once more on Eryk's abandoned cloak. Her fingers brushed against it one last time before she rose, her heart heavy with questions that had no easy answers.

Whatever awaited them deeper in the cavern, she knew one thing for certain—the Frostheart's magic wasn't just powerful. It was dangerous. And her brother was caught at the heart of it.

Chapter 7

The footsteps of the group echoed in the narrow tunnel, and despite the eerie quiet that surrounded them, Liora couldn't shake the gnawing feeling in her gut. The further they went, the more the air seemed to hum with magic. It was as if the Frostheart Stone was pulling them toward it, urging them deeper into the heart of the mountain. It felt like a silent plea to Liora.

"We need to move faster," Kaldor said, his voice low but urgent. His eyes scanned their surroundings with caution. He hadn't said much since they had met Professor Garrick, and Liora couldn't help but feel the tension building between them. His gaze was intense, but his usual calm was slipping. It was as if the very weight of their mission was pressing down on him.

They rounded the corner, and there it was — an opening in the rock, a door made of ice that shimmered faintly in the torchlight. Beyond it, Liora felt the pull of the Stone, growing stronger as though it, too, recognized their presence.

"The Stone lies beyond this door," she murmured. She pulled off her gloves, the cold air biting her fingers as she took a step closer, her outstretched hands hovering before the frosty barrier. Yet, there was something else in the air — something darker. Her face hardened, a flicker of unease passing through her. "But we're not alone."

Professor Gerrick approached the icy door, his fingers grazing its surface with a mix of wonder and reverence. "It will require magic to open," he said, eyes glinting with recognition.

Liora tucked her gloves into her belt, preparing herself for the task at hand. Kaldor's hand rested lightly on her shoulder, a silent gesture of support. "Open the door, and step aside," he said softly, his tone firm. "Let the rest of us go through first, to ensure it's safe."

With a nod, Liora squared her shoulders and stepped forward, confidence settling into her movements. As her hands pressed against the ice, a rush of cold seeped from her fingers, swirling and shimmering in the air before it touched the door, sending a ripple of energy through the frozen surface. The door began to glow faintly as the magic took hold. Finally the frozen doorway gave way, turning inward as if a weight drew it back.

Maren was the first through the door, bow drawn back with an arrow hitched. Following in tight formation was Halric and Rothar. The professor trailing behind in a nervous jog.

"Stay close," Kaldor murmured, his gaze flicking to Liora.

There was a quiet authority in his tone, one that made her want to comply, but she couldn't help the burning pull she felt from the stone.

They entered the chamber cautiously. The room was vast, filled with ancient runes carved into the ice and snow. The Frostheart Stone lay at the center, a pulsating shard of ice barely small enough for a single man of decent strength to carry. It glowed with an otherworldly light. But it wasn't the Stone that drew Liora's attention.

At the far end of the chamber, a group of figures stood in shadow, their voices hushed but unmistakably urgent. The leader, a tall man with a hood obscuring most of his face, spoke first. "The time is almost here," he said. "With the Frostheart Stone in our grasp, we can create the eternal winter. Our power will be unmatched."

Liora's breath caught in her throat. The words echoed in her mind. Eternal winter.

"This is much worse than I thought," she whispered, her eyes widening.

"Exactly," Garrick replied softly, his face a mask of worry. "They're going to use the Stone's power to enslave the realm, to rule it with an iron fist."

Liora felt a wave of anger rise within her. She had always known there were forces at work in the world, but this — this was beyond anything she had imagined. Her brother, Eryk, could very well be involved in this. But could he really have turned against everything they had worked for? Her father's kingdom? The lives of the people who depended on the Stone's protection?

As if sensing her turmoil, Kaldor's hand brushed against hers, and she looked up into his eyes. His gaze was steady, filled with emotion. He was worried about her, she knew that. And as much as she tried to convince herself that the mission was more important, she couldn't ignore the knot tightening in her chest when he looked at her like that.

A sudden noise shattered the moment — a sharp metallic sound of a blade being removed from a metalic sheath. The hooded figures had heard them.

"They know we're here," Kaldor muttered. "Get ready."

Before anyone could react, one of the figures lunged toward them, knocking over a stack of ancient crates, sending them clattering to the floor. The sound reverberated through the chamber, and suddenly, the figures were all in motion, pulling out weapons and moving with the swiftness of trained assassins.

"Attack!" Kaldor yelled, drawing his sword in a fluid, practiced motion.

Liora's heart raced as she unsheathed her own blade. Her magic pulsed beneath her skin, begging to be used, but she knew she had to be careful. The battle wasn't just about survival; it was about staying focused, not losing herself to the panic that threatened to overwhelm her. The ground beneath their feet began to shake and icy stalactites began dropping all around.

Kaldor moved like lightning, his sword flashing in the dim light as he parried a strike from one of the attackers. Liora moved to the side, her feet light on the ice-covered ground. She raised her hand, summoning her magic, and sent a flurry of ice shards spiraling toward the attackers. The sharp sound of cracking ice echoed through the chamber as the shards froze their enemies' weapons to the floor.

"Move!" Kaldor shouted, his eyes locking with hers. He was already moving toward the door as the enemy fled through the other end of the chamber with the stone in hand.

But something was wrong. The shadows in the room were shifting, and Liora could feel the draw of the Frostheart Stone pulling stronger at her as the distance between them grew. She couldn't let them get away. Her brother's fate, the future of Thaldridar—it all tied to this Stone.

"Kaldor, the stone! We have to stop them!" she cried, but he was already moving swiftly toward her, his eyes filled with urgency.

A deep growl of frustration erupted from his lungs as he ran back toward her. "We don't have time!" Kaldor shouted. His voice was hard, filled with that familiar edge. As he reached her, he grabbed her hand, pulling her toward him but she resisted. "The Stone's power is unstable. We need to leave—now!"

But Liora couldn't move. She couldn't let it go. She watched as Kaldor's expression shifted, his protective instincts pushing him forward. "Please, Liora." there it was again. Her name on his lips. It felt more beautiful than any magic she had ever felt before. "I can't lose you."

The words cut through her, and in that moment, she felt a wave of understanding wash over her. This wasn't just about the Stone. This wasn't just about the mission or her brother. It was about something much more profound. Kaldor was scared, scared of losing her, and he was showing it now — perhaps for the first time.

"Let's go," she whispered, glancing back at the Stone one last time.

Kaldor's jaw tightened as he firmly clasped her hand in his. He pulled her close, his arm instinctively shielding her as they made their way toward the exit. Their escape was frantic, the weight of the pursuit on their shoulders. But through the chaos, through the danger, there was a quiet understanding between them — a trust that neither had expected but had grown nonetheless.

As they reached the narrow passage that led to the outside world, Liora glanced over at Kaldor. His expression was completely freed from the walls he had built between them. Having betrayed his hidden feelings for her just moments earlier, there was no way Liora could unsee Kaldor's desire for her.

Everyone bolted out the cave and into the clearing. Kaldor pulled Liora into his arms protectively shielding her from any gusts or falling debris as the ground continued to shake under foot. Liora buried her face inside his cloak, clinging to Kaldor's armor. A large final shudder tossed them all to the snowy ground. Kaldor firmly held onto the princess until the ground stopped shaking.

It was several minutes before Liora heard the others begin to move. She felt Kaldor's head lift from hers but his strong arms remained firmly around her a moment longer.

"Are you alright?" Kaldor's voice was soft but urgent.

Liora lifted her eyes to his. "I will be," Liora answered, her heart pounding in her chest. "But what about Eryk?"

Kaldor paused, his expression unreadable for a moment before he spoke, his voice steady. "We'll find him. And we'll make sure that whatever happens next, we face it together."

They left the cave behind them, and the chill of the mountains surrounded them once again. The snow sprayed up into the air with every step from the Froststeeds — the cold nipping at Liora's fingers — but it was the exhaustion pulling at her bones that worried her more. Her magic was growing stronger with every step — more precise, more potent — but it came at a cost. The strain on her body was becoming undeniable. Every time she tapped into the icy currents of power, it felt as though a part of her was being drained. She wasn't sure how much longer she could sustain it.

"We need to stop them before the Solstice hits," Liora said quietly, her breath swirling in the frigid air. She stole a glance at Kaldor, noticing the grim set of his jaw. He was just as determined as she was, but she could see the toll the journey was taking on her. He hadn't said a word, but the concern in his eyes never wavered.

"We will," Kaldor replied, his gaze fixed on the path ahead.

He didn't look at her when he spoke, but his words settled in her chest like a promise — a promise that both comforted and terrified her.

Kaldor brought his horse to a halt, and the others followed suit. He turned to face his men. "Holric," he called in a commanding tone.

"Sir," the guard replied.

"I want you to take the professor back to the city. The two of you go to the king and report what you've witnessed. We're about a day's ride from Bluhurst Canyon. I believe that's where our enemy will be holed up by the time we catch up to them. Ask the king to send reinforcements."

Liora's brow furrowed as she glanced between them. "Will there be enough time?"

"If they make haste."

"Yes, Sir." Holric nodded, spurring his horse to turn.

"Wait." Liora urged her horse to trot back toward them. She looked directly at Professor Gerrick. "I need you to deliver another message to my father."

"Of course, Princess."

Liora took a deep breath, knowing the confrontation was inevitable. "My father will be angry that I left the castle, and he might even hold Kaldor responsible. When he begins to blame him for not leaving me behind, I need you to remind him that I gave my loyal captain no choice but to bring me along. And make sure to emphasize that it was a good thing I did, as my magic was needed more than once."

"I will do my best, Your Majesty," Gerrick said with a bow,

his voice steady.

Liora gave a sharp nod, watching as he and Holric turned to ride back toward the city.

Chapter 8

As the small caravan trudged through the snow-laden valley, the stillness was shattered by a gut-wrenching scream echoing from within the trees. The sound was raw and visceral, the unmistakable cry of someone in excruciating pain. It sent a chill down Liora's spine that had nothing to do with the winter air.

Liora spun around, her gloved hand instinctively reaching for the hilt of her dagger. Beside her, Kaldor and the other guards drew their weapons in unison, their movements swift and purposeful. Without hesitation, they positioned themselves in a protective line between Liora and the shadowy forest, their sharp eyes scanning the dense thicket for any sign of danger.

Kaldor met her gaze, his expression dark. "Stay behind me."

Liora nodded.

They pushed forward, each step crunching loudly in the snow. The cries grew louder — pained and desperate. They reached a clearing in the trees where the ground dropped into a dry gully. The scene below them made Liora's blood run cold.

A man was kneeling in the snow, his hands bound behind his back. His face was battered, his hair matted with blood. Prince Eryk. Beside him, stood an assassin they had fought hours earlier in the cave — his hand clamped tightly around Eryk's shoulder. The assassin's face twisted into a sneer when he saw them.

"Liora," Eryk rasped, his voice barely audible. "Kaldor…"

"Eryk!" Liora dropped her reins to dismount, but Kaldor's hand shot out, stopping her.

"Careful," Kaldor warned. His voice was calm, but his body was coiled, ready to spring into action. "Let him go," he called to the assassin, his tone icy and authoritative.

The assassin chuckled, his grip on Eryk tightening. "You're too late," he taunted. "The prince is mine. A gift from the Winter King for my assistance in retrieving the stone."

Kaldor, Rothar, and Maren dismounted their horses.

"You won't leave here alive," Kaldor growled, unsheathing his sword in one swift motion.

The assassin's smirk faltered as he pulled Eryk to his feet, using him as a shield. "Take another step, and I'll finish him."

Liora's magic flared at her fingertips, but the sight of her brother's beaten face made her hesitate. "Please," she said, her voice breaking. "He's done nothing to you. Let him go."

The assassin's eyes narrowed. "Done nothing? He betrayed you all. The prince's hands are as dirty as mine. He helped take the Frostheart Stone."

"No," Liora whispered, her heart sinking. She turned to Eryk, desperate for him to deny it. "Eryk... tell me he's lying."

Eryk's gaze dropped to the snow, his silence cutting deeper than any blade. "Liora... I—"

"Enough!" Kaldor barked, his sword flashing as he stepped forward. "Whatever his involvement, the Stone doesn't belong to you."

The assassin shoved Eryk aside, drawing his twin daggers in one fluid motion. "Then come take it from me."

The battle was chaos. The assassin moved like a shadow, his twin daggers flashing in the storm's dim light, each strike swift and deadly. Kaldor met him head-on, his sword clashing against the daggers in a flurry of sparks. His movements were precise, his broad frame an unyielding barrier between the assassin and Liora.

To Kaldor's right, Rothar surged forward, his massive axe swinging with brutal force. The assassin twisted to evade, but Rothar's strikes came with the power of a battering ram, forcing him to retreat a step.

Above them, Maren stood on a snow-covered ridge, her bow drawn taut. She loosed arrow after arrow, her aim deadly. Each shot forced the assassin to move defensively, splitting his attention between Kaldor, Rothar, and the projectiles flying toward him. When she ran out of arrows, she didn't hesitate to leap down, drawing her single sword and joining the fray with nimble precision.

Liora stood just behind them, her heart pounding as she watched the coordinated assault. The icy magic at her fingertips crackled and shimmered, but her fear — fear for Kaldor, for Rothar and Maren, and for her brother — made her hesitate. The assassin's speed was terrifying, his every movement calculated to exploit even the smallest weakness. Clenching her fists, Liora forced herself to focus. They needed her magic, and hesitation wasn't an option. Taking a deep breath, she steadied her trembling hands and unleashed the icy power within her, striking the enemy with long shards of ice — one in the thigh and the other grazing his cheek.

Eryk crawled toward his sister, his face pale and streaked with blood. Grabbing up her skirt, Liora climbed down to him and held him in her arms.

"I didn't want this," he choked out. "They — they had her."

"Her?" Liora demanded, her magic crackling around her. "Who, Eryk?"

Eryk's voice broke. "Alina. They have her, Liora. They said they'd kill her if I didn't help them."

Liora's chest tightened at the mention of Alina, the princess of Eldara. Her brother's betrothal to the future queen of their neighboring kingdom had been celebrated across the land — a union that would strengthen ties between Thaldridar and Eldara for generations to come. She had seen the way Eryk looked at Alina, with a devotion that bordered on reverence.

"They're using her to control you," Liora said, her voice

trembling with anger and fear. "Why didn't you come to me? To Father?"

Eryk shook his head, his tears freezing against his battered cheeks. "There wasn't time. They sent me proof—her ring, her letters—and warned me not to tell anyone. I thought... I thought I could fix it before it came to this."

Liora's magic surged violently as fury swept through her, but Kaldor's voice broke through the haze. "Liora! Now!"

She raised her hands, ice surging forth in a dazzling arc. The magic struck the assassin's legs, freezing him in place. Kaldor wasted no time. His blade sliced cleanly through the man's chest, and the assassin crumpled to the ground, lifeless.

The silence that followed was deafening. Liora fell to her knees beside Eryk, her heart breaking at the sight of him.

"Why, Eryk?" Liora whispered, her voice trembling as she searched his face.

Eryk's gaze dropped to the snow, his shoulders shaking with the weight of his guilt. "Because I can't live without her," he said hoarsely, his voice cracking. "I love her, Liora. More than I ever thought possible."

The confession hung heavy in the icy air. Liora's heart clenched at the raw vulnerability in her brother's voice. She had always known Eryk's feelings for Alina ran deep—his courtship with the princess of Eldara had been more than a political alliance. It had been genuine, passionate, and undeniable. But hearing him admit it so plainly, so brokenly, made the cost of his choices all the more devastating.

Kaldor stepped closer, his sword lowered but still in

hand. His sharp gaze flicked between Liora and Eryk before settling on the prince. "A love like that is rare," he said, his tone measured, though not without empathy. "I just hope the sacrifice you've made for it will withstand the test of time."

Eryk's jaw tightened, and he met Kaldor's eyes. "You think I don't know that? I would do anything to protect her, even if it meant betraying everything else."

The weight of his words struck Liora like a blow. "And now you've put her—and all of us—at even greater risk," she said, her voice sharper than she intended. "Eryk, what were you thinking?"

"I was thinking I could save her!" Eryk snapped, his voice rising. "I thought I could fix everything before it spiraled out of control. But they were always one step ahead. I didn't know how deep this went."

"Enough," Kaldor interjected, his tone firm but not unkind. "What's done is done. Right now, we need to focus on what's ahead."

Liora and Kaldor's eyes met, a silent understanding passing between them. There was no time to dwell on mistakes—only the path forward mattered now.

Kaldor sheathed his sword with a decisive motion and turned to Liora. "We need to move. There's a chance they'll use the Frostheart Stone soon, and when they do, the storm it unleashes will be unstoppable."

Liora nodded, though her mind was still spinning. She reached out to Eryk, her magic instinctively rising to steady him as he swayed on his feet. "We'll save her, Eryk," she said, her voice firm and resolute. "And we'll fix this."

Eryk's eyes glistened with gratitude, though shame still lingered in his features. He didn't trust himself to speak, simply nodding as he leaned into her support.

Kaldor's gaze lingered on Liora, his features softening for the briefest moment. "Together," he said quietly, his voice steady but laced with an unspoken promise.

Chapter 9

The wind screamed around them as if the mountains themselves were wailing in protest. The storm was no longer just weather; it had become a living force — a manifestation of the Frostheart Stone's corrupted magic, lashing out against anyone who dared approach. Liora's breaths came in shallow gasps, each one crystallizing in the frigid air. Her body felt like lead, weighed down by exhaustion and the strain of her magic. Yet she pushed on, her resolve unyielding.

Beside her, Kaldor was a silent wall of strength. His hand hovered near the hilt of his sword, his sharp eyes scanning the blizzard for danger. Behind them, Prince Eryk trudged forward, his steps uneven but determined. His battered face bore the weight of regret, but his resolve to set things right burned brighter than the fury of the storm. Maren and Rothar made up the front and back of their small expedition.

"We're close," Kaldor said, his voice steady despite the chaos. "The clearing is just ahead."

Liora glanced back at her brother. His silence spoke volumes, but she could see the pain etched in every line of his face. He had risked everything to save Alina and in doing so, had unwittingly plunged their kingdom into peril. She wanted to hate him for the betrayal, for keeping his secret until it was too late. But now, all she could feel was determination.

The blizzard began to thin as they reached the ridge, revealing the clearing below. The Frostheart Stone stood at its center, its once-pure glow now fractured and sinister. The dark light pulsed in rhythmic waves, distorting the air around it and feeding the storm's ferocity. Shadows moved around the Stone — figures draped in heavy cloaks, their faces obscured by hoods.

Liora froze, her heart pounding. The conspirators. And at their center stood the leader, but it wasn't The Winter King as they had been told. It was an unknown man his hands raised high as he drew power from the Stone.

"The Stone belongs to us now," the leader called out, his voice cutting through the wind like a blade. "You are too late."

Kaldor's hand tightened on his sword. "Stay back," he warned Liora and Eryk, his tone brooking no argument. "We'll handle this."

Liora stepped forward, ignoring his command. "Yes, all of us will," she corrected, her magic sparking at her fingertips.

Her gaze locked on the Frostheart Stone. The dark magic coursing through it was palpable, a suffocating presence that seemed to pull the air from her lungs. "If they push the Stone any further, it will shatter," she murmured. "And if that happens…"

"The kingdom will freeze," Kaldor finished grimly. "And there'll be no saving it."

From the clearing, the leader laughed, a cold, hollow sound. "You think you can stop us?" he sneered. "The Stone's true power lies in its corruption. With it, we will bring eternal winter and rule the realm."

"You don't know what you're doing!" Liora shouted, stepping closer. The frost swirling around her flared brighter, the magic within her reacting to the Stone's corrupted energy. "The Frostheart Stone isn't a weapon. It's part of the land – it balances Thaldridar. If you destroy it, you destroy everything."

"Then so be it," the leader growled, raising his hands. "You won't live to see the kingdom fall."

With a sharp motion, he unleashed a wave of dark magic toward them. Kaldor was already moving, his sword flashing as he stepped in front of Liora, deflecting the attack. "Eryk, stay behind her!" he barked, his voice like steel.

Maren and Rothar charged toward the oncoming enemies with calculated movements.

"Liora, the Stone. You're the only one who can stop it," Kaldor called out.

Liora nodded, her heart pounding. She could feel the Stone's pull, its corrupted power clashing against her own magic. She had to purify it — to restore its balance before it was too late, but there was still a chance that the stone wouldn't accept her magic. If the Frostheart Stone didn't accept the princess as its guardian, then all would be lost anyway. She pushed the thought away. They had come too far to let such thoughts deter her from doing everything she could to save her people.

Drawing a deep breath, she raised her hands, summoning the frost within her. Ice spiraled outward, weaving intricate patterns in the air as it surged toward the Stone. But the leader wasn't done. He directed another wave of dark magic, this time aimed at Liora.

Kaldor leapt into its path, his sword absorbing the brunt of the blow. He staggered but didn't fall, his fierce gaze locking on the leader. "Keep going, Liora!" he shouted, his voice raw with determination.

She focused, pushing her magic further. The frost reached the Stone, wrapping around its fractured surface in a shimmering cocoon. The dark magic recoiled, resisting her efforts, but she refused to let go. Her chest ached with the strain, her vision blurring as she poured every ounce of strength into the purification.

Maren and Rothar moved in toward the stone, doing everything they could to keep the opposing side from coming near it while the princess worked her magic.

Eryk stood protectively beside her, his eyes darting between the Stone and the conspirators. He clenched his fists, frustration written across his battered face. "What can I do?" he asked, his voice strained. "Liora, tell me how to help."

"Keep them away from the Stone!" she managed, her voice trembling with effort.

Eryk grabbed a fallen dagger from the snow, stepping in front of her. His movements were clumsy, but his resolve was unshakable. When one of the conspirators charged toward them, Eryk met him head-on, the clash of blades ringing out against the storm.

Kaldor dispatched another attacker, his movements precise and deadly. The leader snarled, gathering more power from the Stone in a desperate bid to maintain control. The air crackled with energy as dark and light clashed, the storm raging around them with renewed ferocity.

"Liora!" Kaldor's voice cut through the chaos, drawing her focus. His eyes met hers, and in that moment, the world seemed to still. "You can do this," he said, his voice steady despite the storm. "I believe in you."

Her heart swelled with his words, and for the first time, she felt a flicker of hope. Drawing on the last reserves of her magic, she thrust her hands forward, pouring everything into the Frostheart Stone. The frost surged, engulfing the Stone completely.

The dark magic fought back, writhing as if it were a living, vengeful creature. Liora's hands trembled, her entire body straining under the force of its resistance. Still, she pushed harder, her icy magic surging with unwavering resolve. The corruption encasing the Frostheart Stone began to crack, fractures spidering through its tainted glow as the pure magic fought to reclaim its place.

With a final, blinding flash of light, the dark energy shattered, dissipating into the storm in shimmering fragments. The air stilled, and the Stone's glow returned to its original brilliance—a soft, steady blue that pulsed with life and hope. The Stone's magic surged through her, warm and unyielding, a silent acknowledgment. The Frostheart Stone had accepted her as its guardian.

"No!" A scornful cry erupted from the enemy leader, his voice cutting through the moment of triumph like a blade. His expression twisted with fury as he lunged, his weapon aimed at Kaldor's unguarded back.

"Kaldor!" Liora's warning rang out, but before the enemy could strike, a whistle cut through the air. Maren's arrow found its mark, burying itself deep in the man's neck. His momentum faltered, and he crumpled to the ground, the weapon slipping from his lifeless hand. The snow beneath him turned crimson, the vivid color stark against the pristine white. For a breathless moment, silence reigned, save for the faint hum of the Frostheart Stone's magic.

Seeing their leader fall, the remaining conspirators faltered. Their resolve broke, and without so much as a backward glance, they scattered in all directions, abandoning both their fallen leader and their claim to the Stone. Liora's chest heaved as she watched them flee, the weight of what they had accomplished settling over her.

"It's over," Kaldor said, his voice steady but edged with exhaustion. He turned to her, his gaze meeting hers. "We did it."

Liora's breaths came in shallow gasps as she leaned against Kaldor, her body trembling from the effort of cleansing the Stone. The frost magic within her had gone quiet, leaving an ache in its absence, but she didn't regret a moment of it. They had won.

Maren began retrieving what arrows she could find around them. As she passed by Kaldor he placed a hand on her shoulder and she stopped at his side. "Thank you," he said with a meaningful stare.

"Just one tally mark I can cross off from all of the times you've had my back, Captain," she replied.

Eryk stood a few steps away, staring at the Frostheart Stone. Relief softened his features, but a flicker of anxiety remained in his eyes. The victory felt incomplete. "Alina," he whispered, her name like a prayer on the wind.

And then they heard it—a faint, muffled cry carried through the stillness.

Eryk's head snapped up, his breath catching in his throat. "Alina!" he shouted, spinning toward the sound. He and Rothar sprinted across the snow—Eryk's battered form moving with a desperation that only love could fuel.

"Eryk, wait!" Liora called after him, her voice hoarse. But Kaldor's steady hand on her shoulder stopped her from following.

"Let him go," Kaldor said softly. His gaze followed Eryk, his expression unreadable. "He needs this."

The two men disappeared into the trees, the crunch of their hurried footsteps fading into the distance. The clearing suddenly felt emptier, the weight of everything they had endured settling heavily on Liora's chest. She slumped against Kaldor, letting his warmth steady her.

Moments later, Eryk's voice rang out again, louder this time. "I found her!"

"Oh!" Liora's heart leapt. "Help me, Kaldor," she asked while taking his hand to get to her feet. Together, they followed the sound, their feet moving as quickly as the snow would allow. When they reached Eryk, they saw him kneeling in the snow, cradling Alina in his arms.

The princess of Eldara was bound and shivering, her gown torn and dusted with frost. Tears streaked her cheeks, but she was otherwise unharmed. Her wide eyes lifted to Liora and Kaldor, before returning to Eryk's. Her lips trembled. "Eryk," she whispered, clutching at him like he was her lifeline. "I was so afraid."

"You're safe now," Eryk murmured, his voice thick with emotion. He pulled her closer, pressing his forehead to hers. "I'm so sorry, Alina. I should have stopped this before it reached you."

"You saved me," Alina said, her voice trembling. "That's all that matters."

Liora's heart clenched as she watched the two of them. The love between them was undeniable, their bond forged through trials neither should have had to endure. She exchanged a glance with Kaldor, who stood silent and still, his expression carefully neutral.

"We need to get her somewhere warm," Kaldor said, his

voice breaking the moment. "She's been in the cold too long."

Eryk nodded, his movements careful as he helped Alina to her feet. The princess wobbled but leaned into him for support, her breaths visible in the frigid air. "The Frostheart is safe?" she asked, her voice faint.

"It is," Liora said firmly. "The corruption is gone. It's pure again."

Alina's lips parted in relief, her eyes filling with gratitude. "Thank you," she whispered. "You've saved more than just me. You've saved all of us."

Liora felt Kaldor's hand rest lightly on her back, grounding her as she nodded. "We all did."

As they began their trek back to the clearing, the vibrant blue and silver banners of Thaldridar came into view, fluttering proudly in the icy wind. A full legion of the king's army marched toward them, their armor glinting under the pale sunlight. The sight should have brought relief, but Kaldor's scoff of disappointment broke the silence.

"Of course, they arrive now," he muttered, shaking his head. "All too late."

Liora, however, couldn't hold back the laughter that bubbled up from within her. It started as a soft chuckle and quickly grew, her voice ringing out in the crisp air. Kaldor turned toward her, his brow furrowing in confusion, but the sound of her unrestrained joy melted away the irritation he'd felt moments before.

"Really?" he asked, his voice caught between exasperation

and amusement.

"Oh, Kaldor," she managed between laughs, wiping a tear from her cheek. "What am I going to do with you? You act as though the entire kingdom relies solely on your shoulders."

"Well, someone has to be dependable," he replied dryly, but the faintest smile began to tug at his lips.

And then it happened—a laugh, deep and genuine, escaped him. It startled even himself, and Liora's eyes widened in delight. As his laughter grew, his usual stoic expression gave way to a bright, unguarded smile. It was the first time Liora had ever seen him like this, and it made her heart skip.

"That's it!" she exclaimed, pointing at him with mock triumph. "I've done it! I've finally made you smile a real genuine smile."

Kaldor shook his head, his laugh trailing into a warm chuckle. "You're insufferable, Princess."

"And you're not as humorless as you pretend to be," she teased, grinning up at him.

For a moment, the weariness of their journey and the tension of battle faded, replaced by a shared sense of triumph—not just in their survival, but in finding lightness in the midst of it all. The sight of Kaldor's rare, genuine smile only made the moment sweeter, and for Liora, it felt like the beginning of something new.

Chapter 10

The ride back to the capital was triumphant. The storm that had raged for days had finally calmed, leaving a soft blanket of snow across the land. The silence was broken only by the crunch of hooves on frost-covered ground and the occasional murmurs between Eryk and Alina. The Thaldridarian army stretched far behind them, with soldiers forming a protective detail at the front and flanking either side of the caravan. At the head rode Kaldor, Maren, and Rothar, with Liora close by, her thoughts churning as the city's spires came into view.

The Frostheart Stone, now restored to its rightful state, rested securely in Kaldor's satchel. Its gentle glow had returned—a beacon of hope for Thaldridar—yet Liora couldn't shake the lingering weight of its power, an unspoken reminder of the trials they had endured.

Eryk remained close to Alina, steadying her on her horse. Though she was safe, the ordeal had left her pale and quiet, her once-bright eyes shadowed with fear. Eryk, too, bore the scars of his choices, but his unwavering gaze rarely left Alina's face. Their bond had deepened in ways no political alliance or formal courtship could match.

Liora glanced back at them, her heart softening. Whatever anger she had harbored toward her brother had melted away, replaced by an understanding she hadn't expected. Eryk had made mistakes, but they had been born of love — a love worth fighting for.

"They'll be all right," Kaldor said quietly, his voice breaking through her thoughts.

Liora turned to him, studying his profile in the soft dawn light. There was a tension in the set of his jaw and the way he gripped the reins. "Do you really believe that?" she asked softly.

Kaldor nodded, his expression steady. "They've endured more than most would in a lifetime. That kind of love doesn't break easily."

She couldn't tell if he was speaking about Eryk and Alina or something else entirely, but his words warmed her nonetheless.

As they approached the outskirts of the city, the sight awaiting them was both humbling and awe-inspiring. Along the road, banners bearing the crest of Thaldridar fluttered in the crisp air. At the forefront, mounted on a steed as imposing as its rider, was the king. Clad in full battle armor that gleamed under the pale winter light, he looked every bit the warrior of old—a commanding presence that brought both reassurance and gravity to the moment.

It had been many years since Liora had seen her father dressed for battle. The sight stirred a mix of pride, awe, and uncertainty within her.

"Father!" Eryk's voice rang out as he spurred his horse into a gallop toward the king.

The king's stern expression softened as he saw his son approach, though the relief in his eyes was tempered by the weight of all that had transpired. As Eryk dismounted, the king leaned forward to clasp his shoulder with a firm, fatherly grip.

"You are safe," the king said, his steady voice carrying a depth of emotion. "But there is much to discuss."

Eryk nodded, his features somber. "Yes, there is."

Liora slid gracefully from her Froststeed, her boots crunching softly against the snow as she stepped closer. She exchanged a glance with Kaldor, unspoken understanding passing between them. They had won this battle, but the war against the conspirators was far from over. The darkness that had fueled the plot still loomed, its reach yet unknown.

The king's gaze found Liora next, lingering. She couldn't quite tell if he looked at her with pride or disapproval, though she felt she deserved a measure of both.

"Captain," the king said, his tone carrying the authority of his station as he turned his attention to Kaldor. "I appreciate you bringing my children home to me."

Kaldor inclined his head, his deep voice unwavering. "The mission would have failed without the bravery of Princess Liora, Your Highness. Much of our success is due to her resolve and skill—most especially in retrieving the Frostheart Stone."

The king's gaze shifted back to his daughter, a quiet softness replacing his earlier scrutiny. "Yes, I've heard of some of her... adventures," he said, his tone light but laced with solemnity. "You have made your people very proud, daughter."

A faint warmth spread through Liora's chest at his words, but it was tempered by the weight of what she needed to say. She lifted her chin, her blue eyes meeting his with quiet resolve. "Father, there's something else you should know," she began, her voice steady despite the enormity of the revelation.

The king's brow furrowed slightly, his attention sharpening. "Go on."

Liora took a measured breath, her hands clasping in front of her. "The Frostheart Stone... it has accepted me as its guardian. The magic, the responsibility—it's mine now."

For a moment, silence hung between them, the significance of her words settling like a tangible weight in the air. The king's expression shifted, a flicker of surprise crossing his features before it was replaced by something deeper—pride mingled with understanding.

"It chose you," he said softly, almost to himself. His gaze grew warmer, though his voice retained its gravity. "You have taken on a great burden, Liora. One that only the strongest of hearts can bear."

"I'm ready," she replied with quiet determination, though the truth was, she still wasn't entirely sure. But she knew she had to be. For the kingdom, for her family, and for herself.

The king nodded slowly, his demeanor softening further. "Then Thaldridar is in good hands, my daughter. Yours and yours alone."

Liora's chest swelled with emotion, but she didn't let it overwhelm her. Instead, she offered him a small, resolute smile, silently vowing not to falter under the weight of her new role.

Straightening in his saddle, the king raised his voice to address the gathered crowd. "Let it be known that the Frostheart Stone has been returned, and the Princess of Thaldridar has proven herself not only brave and worthy, but has also been ordained as the Guardian of the Frostheart!"

A cheer erupted from the crowd, their voices carrying warmth that defied the wintry air. For the first time in days, Liora felt a sense of home settle over her. Yet even as she let the relief wash over her, she knew there was still work to be done.

It was the eve of the Winter Solstice, and the grand hall had been transformed into a breathtaking winter wonderland. Evergreen garlands intertwined with silver and blue ribbons adorned the towering pillars, their fragrance mingling with the aromas of spiced cider and roasted chestnuts. Frosted glass lanterns cast a magical glow, while enchanted snowflakes twinkled lazily in the air.

A massive evergreen tree stood at the hall's center, its

glittering ice ornaments reflecting the flickering light. Beneath it, elaborately wrapped gifts awaited honored guests. Nobles in jeweled winter finery mingled with knights in polished armor, merchants exchanged stories with scholars, and children's laughter echoed as harpists played softly. At the head of the hall, the royal family's dais shimmered with banners bearing Thaldridar's crest—a snowflake entwined with a blade—a proud symbol of strength and unity.

Everywhere Liora looked, the hall shimmered with celebration, the joy of the Winter Solstice filling every corner. Dignitaries from across the kingdom approached her throughout the evening, each offering their gratitude for her bravery and recounting the tales they'd heard of her recent triumphs. She smiled graciously, offering polite words in return, but her heart wasn't in it.

Her thoughts were elsewhere, her eyes scanning the room inconspicuously, though her focus never lingered long before she was drawn into another conversation. She was beginning to think she wouldn't see him at all tonight, and the realization unsettled her. Liora had grown so accustomed to Kaldor's steady presence that the thought of his absence left her feeling strangely unfettered.

Liora had seen her father and brother several times throughout the evening, though the king had stepped out for the past little while. Eryk, however, was still making the rounds, engaging with the guests. Princess Alina was notably absent. Her fragile disposition, still shaken by the ordeal she had endured, had left her too overwhelmed to attend the festivities. Not a single person blamed her for wanting to keep to her chambers.

With every passing moment, Liora's unease grew, tinged with frustration. She could almost feel Kaldor's absence like a void in the room, and it made her restless. Surely, he would come — wouldn't he? Why hadn't he sought her out? She tried to ignore the sting of disappointment, but it was no use. Even amidst the glittering decor and warm smiles of her people, Liora's mind was consumed by the one person she wanted to see most.

The sentry sounded their horns, gaining the full attention of everyone at the celebration. A wide berth was made around King Aldryn as he began to address the room.

"The Winter Solstice has always been a spiritual and joyful event for Thaldridar, but tonight we also celebrate the Frostheart Stones return to its rightful place!"

Cheers and applause echoed in response.

The king gestured for quiet before continuing, his gaze turning to Liora's. "The bravery of our people runs deep, but none so deep as Princess Liora. My daughter and the next queen of Thaldridar."

Gasps rippled through the hall, followed by thunderous applause. Liora's chest tightened, her mind spinning. Queen? She had always known this day would come, but not so soon, and not like this.

The walk from where she stood to her father felt like the longest distance she had ever crossed, but she finally made it to him, he embraced her with the warmest hug and a kiss on her forehead.

"You have made me proud," he said with tearfilled eyes.

Liora was speechless. She laid her head on her fathers shoulder and hugged him tight.

The celebrations stretched long into the evening, but Liora slipped away as soon as she could, seeking the solace of the palace gardens. The snow glittered under the moonlight, and the cold air was a welcome reprieve from the stifling warmth of the hall. She didn't hear Kaldor approach until his cloak brushed lightly against hers.

"Here you are," he said softly, his deep voice carrying over the distant hum of the festivities.

Liora smiled faintly but didn't turn to face him right away. "Me? Where were you all night?"

"Letting you and your family have your moment of victory," he replied, his tone laced with humility.

"It was your victory as well," she said, turning slightly to meet his gaze. The warm glow of the lanterns reflected in his deep brown eyes. "Or did you forget the last few days?"

"How could I?" Kaldor murmured, his voice dropping lower. "They changed me in more ways than I thought possible."

Liora spun fully to face him, her fur-lined cloak flaring slightly with the movement. "Evidently not enough if you haven't learned not to leave me unattended."

"What do you mean?" Kaldor asked, his brow furrowing. "You were perfectly safe."

"Captain Kaldor," she growled, stepping closer, her frustration spilling over. "I needed you tonight. I needed your calming presence, your grounding demeanor. Not having you beside me was like missing my right arm—"

Kaldor suddenly grabbed her by the arms, his grip firm yet gentle as he pulled her closer. Their faces were just inches apart, their breaths mingling in soft clouds against the cold air.

Liora's heart pounded wildly in her chest, her lips parting as her eyes searched his. Every inch of her pleaded silently for him to close the space between them.

Kaldor's expression softened, and a flicker of hesitation crossed his features before he slid his arms around her waist, lifting her effortlessly. Her feet dangled above the ground, but in his embrace, she felt anchored.

"May I kiss you?" he asked, his voice a breathless whisper, his forehead resting against hers.

"I wish you would," Liora replied, her voice trembling with anticipation.

The corner of his mouth lifted into a rare, tender smile before he leaned in, his lips brushing against hers in a kiss that was soft yet filled with unspoken passion.

Liora's hands slid up into his hair, her fingers tangling gently as she held onto him, deepening the kiss. A soft sigh escaped her as the world seemed to fade, leaving only the warmth of his touch and the intoxicating closeness between them.

When they finally broke apart, their foreheads remained pressed together, their breaths mingling in the crisp night air.

Kaldor's arms tightened around her, holding her close as if to promise he would never let her go again.

Liora smiled, her heart swelling. "That was worth the wait."

Kaldor chuckled softly, his rare smile lingering. "It won't take that long next time."

"It better not." Liora softly kissed his chin, then each cheek before returning to his soft thick lips.

Chapter 11

The morning sunlight filtered softly through the frosted windows of Thaldridar's bustling city, casting a warm glow over the snow-dusted cobblestones. Liora strolled through the streets, her cloak trailing behind her as she moved from one shop to the next, her bright blue eyes scanning displays of fabrics, jewels, and delicacies. The weight of her upcoming coronation lingered in her thoughts, but today, it felt less like a burden and more like a promise — a step toward the future she was finally ready to embrace.

Kaldor followed her closely. His sharp gaze darted over passersby, ever watchful, but the tension in his posture softened each time Liora's laughter rang out, light and carefree. She was meticulously selecting items for her coronation —

gowns, menus, and gifts for honored guests — but her attention wasn't entirely on the task at hand.

They paused outside a bakery, the scent of spiced pastries wafting into the street. Liora tilted her head toward Kaldor with a playful smile. "What do you think? Cinnamon or honey glaze for the morning feast?"

He raised a brow, his lips twitching into a faint smile. "I think the guests will be happy with whatever you choose, Princess."

Liora leaned closer, her hand brushing his briefly as she reached for a sample offered by the baker. The warmth of his fingers lingered on hers, sending a quiet thrill through her even as she tried to appear composed. She glanced up at him, catching the soft flicker of affection in his deep brown eyes before he quickly returned his attention to the crowd.

As they moved to the tailor's shop, Kaldor held the door open for her, inhaling the diving essence of her scent as she passed.

Liora busied herself with bolts of fabric and intricate embroidery patterns. "This one," she said, holding up a shimmering blue cloth that mirrored the hue of her eyes. "What do you think?"

Kaldor stepped closer, his gaze dropping from the fabric to her face. His voice was low, meant only for her. "It's perfect. It suits you."

The subtle intimacy of his tone made her heart flutter, but she hid it behind a playful smile. "You'd say that about anything I chose."

"Only if it were true," he replied, his expression unreadable, though his eyes lingered on hers a moment too long.

They continued their walk through the city, the vibrant hum of life surrounding them. Vendors called out their wares, children darted through the streets, and the distant melody of a lute carried on the crisp air. The people greeted them warmly — nobles bowing respectfully, merchants offering their congratulations, and common folk flashing beaming smiles.

"Princess Liora!" an older woman exclaimed, bowing deeply. "May the gods bless you on your coronation. You are truly the heart of Thaldridar."

"Thank you," Liora said graciously, her voice warm. But even as she acknowledged the woman, her thoughts were on Kaldor. Every shared glance, every fleeting touch, felt like a stolen moment — a secret only they understood.

When they paused near a jeweler's stall, Kaldor stepped beside her, his voice soft. "You haven't stopped smiling all morning."

She glanced up at him, her expression radiant. "How could I not? Everything feels... different now."

Kaldor's hand brushed hers as they admired a delicate crown adorned with frost-like gemstones. "For the better, I hope," he said, his voice low enough that only she could hear.

"For the better," she agreed, her fingers lingering near his for a heartbeat longer than propriety allowed.

It was in those quiet, stolen moments, Liora felt a lightness she hadn't known in years. And though the people around them might have thought she was focused on her future as queen, her thoughts were firmly rooted in the man who walked steadfastly at her side.

She looked up at him, noting how relaxed he seemed today — how different from the captain of the guard who had stood with his stoic expression through all of their trials. Now, with the weight of their mission over and the kingdom at peace for the moment, Kaldor was smiling more, teasing her in ways that made her heart flutter. She couldn't help but laugh at his easy manner as he playfully bumped her shoulder.

"You know," Liora said, her voice light, "I think you've gotten a little too comfortable with this whole 'smiling' thing. I'm not sure the old Kaldor would approve."

Kaldor chuckled, the sound rich and warm. "Maybe I'm just happy that we've survived this madness. I've always been more comfortable around swords than I am around smiles. But you... you've always had a way of making everything seem brighter."

Liora's smile softened, and she squeezed his hand. "I'm glad I could help," she teased, her voice low and teasing.

They continued to walk through the city, their banter a welcome escape from the weight of everything they'd endured. There was no talk of the conspirators left in hiding, no worry about the kingdom's future. For a few brief moments, everything felt normal again, as it should have been.

But as they reached the outskirts of the city, Kaldor slowed his pace, his eyes growing distant. Liora noticed the shift, the subtle change in the air. She glanced up at him, sensing the gravity of the moment.

The late afternoon sun cast a warm golden glow across the snow-dusted gardens as Kaldor led Liora through the quiet outskirts of the city. The cobblestone path wound toward a secluded spot she hadn't visited since she was a child — a stone gazebo nestled among evergreen trees. Its frosted arches shimmered in the light, delicate icicles hanging from its edges like nature's adornments.

Liora glanced up at him, a curious smile tugging at her lips. "Where are you taking me?"

"You'll see," he said, his tone laced with an unusual softness. His hand rested lightly on hers as they walked, a gesture she'd come to treasure in their stolen moments together.

When they reached the gazebo, Liora gasped softly. The stone pillars seemed almost alive, the sunlight refracting off the ice in a dazzling display. Inside, the snow had been swept away, leaving the space pristine and inviting. A single bench rested at the center, its surface lined with a blanket of deep blue, the royal color of Thaldridar.

"Kaldor," she whispered, turning to him. "This is beautiful."

He smiled faintly, his dark-streaked platinum hair catching the light as he stepped closer. "Not as beautiful as you," he said simply, the words carrying a weight that made her heart skip.

Kaldor turned to her, his expression serious now. The teasing, the easy banter — all of it seemed to melt away.

Liora's heart skipped a beat, sensing the shift in his mood.

"Kaldor?" she asked, her voice tinged with curiosity.

He took a step closer, taking both of her hands in his. "Liora," he began, his voice steady but filled with an intensity she hadn't heard before. "I've spent so long trying to keep my feelings locked away, trying to hide them behind duty and responsibility. But I can't do that anymore. Not with you."

Her heart pounded in her chest as she looked up at him, her thoughts swirling. Her breath caught in her throat. "Kaldor," she whispered, her voice barely audible.

He smiled, but there was a vulnerability in his eyes that Liora hadn't seen before. He dropped to one knee in front of her, holding up a small velvet pouch. "No matter where I am or what I'm doing," Kaldor said, stepping closer, his deep brown eyes holding hers with an intensity that stole her breath. "My heart will always belong to you. You're not just my queen — you're the only one who will ever rule my heart. Would you do me the great honor of marrying me?"

Tears filled her eyes, catching the soft light that danced around them, and her breath hitched in her throat. This moment — this beautiful, perfect moment — felt like the culmination of every trial, every heartache, every victory. It had all led her here, to Kaldor.

"I — I don't know what to say," she whispered, her voice trembling as emotion threatened to overwhelm her.

Kaldor's lips curved into a tender smile, his thumb brushing gently over her hand, sending warmth rippling through her. "You don't have to say anything," he murmured, his voice steady yet filled with vulnerability. "Except yes.

Please, say yes."

The sincerity in his words, the way his deep brown eyes searched hers for the answer, made her heart ache in the best way. The world around them faded away as she let the moment settle between them, her fingers curling instinctively around his. The tears that had filled her eyes spilled over as she pressed her lips against his.

"Yes," she breathed. "Yes, Kaldor. A thousand times yes."

Kaldor's laughter, warm and full of relief, filled the air as he lifted her off the ground, spinning her in his arms. She clung to him, laughing through her tears.

He set her down gently, his hands framing her face as he gazed into her eyes. The storm that had raged in both their lives for so long had finally calmed, and in that stillness, they found something even more powerful.

Their lips met in a deep, beautiful kiss that spoke of all the love they had yet to express. It was the beginning of something new — something they would build together.

As their lips parted, Liora leaned forward, her forehead resting gently against his, their breaths mingling in the frosty air. "You've always been my protector," she whispered, her voice soft and full of emotion. "Now, you'll be my king."

Kaldor's smile deepened, his eyes brimming with unwavering devotion. "Fitting," he murmured, his hand caressing her cheek, "as you've always been the queen of my heart."

The world seemed to fade around them, leaving only the two of them, standing in the peaceful garden as snowflakes drifted gently from the sky. Liora knew, without a doubt, that their journey together was just beginning.

THE END

Enjoy the book?

You can support the author by leaving a review on Amazon, Goodreads, and BookBub.

Subscribe to C. N. Noble's newsletter so you don't miss out on any upcoming news!

About the Author

C. N. Noble spent over twenty years as a closet writer before bravely stepping out of her introverted comfort zone. She is happily married and enjoys spending time with family, reading, gaming, gardening, walking in the woods, and pretending to have a social life. She's a high-functioning introvert who hides from unexpected guests, except for the UPS guy, who brings her book swag.

www.ingramcontent.com/pod-product-compliance
Lightning Source LLC
Chambersburg PA
CBHW060235180626
46813CB00007B/3092